The Chocolate Rose

READ ALL THE CANDY FAIRIES BOOKS!

Chocolate Dreams

Rainbow Swirl

Caramel Moon

Cool Mint

Magic Hearts

Gooey Goblins

The Sugar Ball

A Valentine's Surprise

Bubble Gum Rescue

Double Dip

Jelly Bean Jumble

COMING SOON:

A Royal Wedding

Candy Fairies

The Chocolate Rose

HELEN PERELMAN

ILLUSTRATED BY
ERICA-JANE WATERS

ALADDIN
NEW YORK   LONDON   TORONTO   SYDNEY   NEW DELHI

ALADDIN

An imprint of Simon & Schuster Children's Publishing Division

1230 Avenue of the Americas, New York, NY 10020

First Aladdin paperback edition July 2013

Text copyright © 2013 by Helen Perelman

Illustrations copyright © 2013 by Erica-Jane Waters

All rights reserved, including the right of reproduction in whole or in part in any form.

ALADDIN is a trademark of Simon & Schuster, Inc., and related logo is a registered
trademark of Simon & Schuster, Inc.

Also available in an Aladdin hardcover edition.

For information about special discounts for bulk purchases, please contact

Simon & Schuster Special Sales at 1-866-506-1949 or business@simonandschuster.com.

The Simon & Schuster Speakers Bureau can bring authors to your live event.

For more information or to book an event contact the Simon & Schuster

Speakers Bureau at 1-866-248-3049 or visit our website at www.simonspeakers.com.

Designed by Karina Granda

The text of this book was set in Berthold Baskerville Book.

Manufactured in the United States of America 0613 OFF

2 4 6 8 10 9 7 5 3 1

Library of Congress Control Number 2013937572

ISBN 978-1-4424-5299-2 (pbk)

ISBN 978-1-4424-6499-5 (hc)

ISBN 978-1-4424-5300-5 (eBook)

To my mom,
who loves chocolate

Contents

1

The Seeds

Cocoa the Chocolate Fairy woke up early. She stretched her golden wings and looked out her window. She was eager to get outside and check on her garden.

Just a few weeks ago Cocoa had visited her older cousin Mocha, and her cousin had given her special chocolate flower seedlings to plant in her own garden. Every day for the last week, Cocoa woke up extra early to see if the buds were opening. Maybe today the seedlings would flower!

Mocha had a real gift with flowers. Her garden was known far and wide for its beauty and the vivid colors of each blossom. She lived in Sugar Kingdom and had a very important job: She was the chief gardener and tended to the Royal Palace's flowers for King Crunch and Queen Sweetie, Princess Lolli and Princess Sprinkle's parents. Cocoa was so proud of her!

When Cocoa reached her garden, she was happy to see little stems peeking through the brown-sugar soil.

"Good morning," she said to the seedlings.

She bent down and watered the tiny chocolate stems with her watering can. Carefully, she sprinkled water on the center flower. This was a chocolate rose.

"You are doing just fine," she whispered to the tiny seedling. "I will take care of you. Mocha told me what to do."

Normally, chocolate roses did not bloom in Sugar Valley, but Cocoa was determined to grow one. The first thing she did when she came home from visiting Mocha was plant the seedlings. She spread chocolate sprinkles around the stems just as she had seen Mocha do.

Cocoa sat down on a large rock candy next to the garden and admired her work. She had cleared the flower bed herself. She had turned the sugar soil and put rock candy along the edges. Cocoa dreamed of having a garden filled with flowers. The garden was not as fancy as the ones at the king and queen's palace or at Mocha's, but this garden was all hers.

"*Sweeeeeeet* morning!" a voice called from above.

Cocoa looked up and saw her Caramel Fairy friend. Melli's wings were fluttering fast. Cocoa could tell that Melli was bursting with news.

"What's the good word?" Cocoa called.

Melli came swooping down. Her excitement made her wings move quickly, and she floated above Cocoa.

"Princess Lolli's parents, King Crunch and Queen Sweetie, are coming to Candy Kingdom!" Melli exclaimed.

"The king and queen are coming *here*?" Cocoa asked. She had never met the royal couple. She knew them from their large portraits in Princess Lolli's throne room. They looked like sweet and kind fairies. A visit from them was a very big deal! "Princess Lolli must be so excited that her parents are coming," she added.

"She is," Melli told her. "In honor of their visit, there is going to be a royal talent show on the shore of Chocolate River." Melli did a flip in the air. "How sweet is that?"

"A talent show?" Cocoa repeated.

"Princess Lolli thought it would be a great idea," Melli replied. "I think it is a *sugar-tastic* one! Don't you?"

Cocoa's wings twitched.

"All the fairies in the kingdom are being asked to help build the outdoor stage," Melli went on.

"An outdoor stage?" Cocoa asked.

"Yes!" Melli cried. She did a few more flips high in the air. "The show is next week." She landed next to Cocoa and sat down on the rock. "I am going to play my new licorice-stick clarinet!" she said, giggling.

Cocoa smiled at her friend. Melli was too excited to stay still. Even though she was sitting,

her wings were still fluttering. Melli loved playing her licorice-stick. She had been taking lessons, and she practiced all the time. A talent show was the perfect event for her to show off her new instrument. "That is great, Melli," Cocoa said. "You are going to steal the show."

"I don't know about that," Melli said. She leaped up and stood in front of Cocoa. She studied her friend. "What's wrong?"

"Nothing," Cocoa said quickly. "I . . . well . . . I don't—"

"What are you going to do for the show?" Melli asked, interrupting her.

Cocoa looked down at the ground. Her wings drooped. "Oh, I don't know," she said.

Melli looked at her. "How come you don't seem excited about this? All the fairies in the kingdom are buzzing about this news."

Cocoa got up and walked closer to her flowers. "I am," she said. "I am excited to see the king and the queen."

"What about the show?" Melli asked.

"I don't know," Cocoa said softly. She sat back down on the rock.

"I am sure you can do an act with Berry, Raina, or Dash," Melli said quickly. "For sure, they will all want to be a part of this. Who wouldn't want to be in the royal talent show?"

Cocoa watched Melli twirl around. She knew someone who wouldn't want to be center stage—herself! She didn't have the heart to tell Melli. Melli was usually so shy and unsure. Now look at her! She was excited about performing. Cocoa sighed. Melli had real talent and loved playing her instrument. She would be a perfect act.

"We will all be in the show together," Melli went on. "And imagine, we'll get to perform for King Crunch and Queen Sweetie! Princess Lolli will be so proud!"

Cocoa lowered her head. She didn't know how to tell her friend she was not planning on having any part in the event. Thinking about standing onstage in front of all those fairies— and the king and queen—made her heart race. If only she had a musical talent like Melli did! But Cocoa couldn't hum a tune, let alone play an instrument. There was no way she could get onstage to be in the talent show— especially in front of the king and queen!

2

Talent Show Talk

As the sun moved toward the Frosted Mountains, Cocoa got ready for Sun Dip. The day always ended with Sun Dip. All over Sugar Valley, fairies gathered with their friends to share the news of the day. Cocoa had been having Sun Dip with Melli, Raina the Gummy Fairy, Berry the Fruit Fairy, and Dash the

Mint Fairy for as long as she could remember. These fairies were her closest friends, and Sun Dip was an extra-sweet time. But today was different. Cocoa knew she would be the only fairy who was not going to be filled with excitement about the upcoming talent show.

They all know what they will do for an act, Cocoa thought sadly. She flew slowly toward the red sands of Red Licorice Lake. For sure, the talk tonight would be all about the show.

When Cocoa landed, Raina and Dash were already there. As Cocoa had imagined, they were giddy with excitement.

"I can't wait!" Dash cried. "I have a new idea for a dance routine. We can all wear sugarcoated headbands and different-colored jeweled dresses."

"Maybe we should come up with the steps first," Raina said. "It *is* important to learn all the steps of the dance."

Dash pulled out a pad of paper. "I've been making a list of songs for the routine," she said. "Sure as sugar, we should pick a Sugar Pops song."

"Yes!" Raina exclaimed. "Let's see your list."

Cocoa waved to them, but both Raina and Dash were too busy making their plans.

Melli flew in next and gave Cocoa a hug. "Have you thought more about being part of the show?" She raised her eyebrows. "I really hope you'll do it."

Dash turned to Cocoa. "Wait, you are not going to be in our act?"

"We need you," Raina told Cocoa. "I've been planning this dance for *three* fairies."

Cocoa wasn't sure what to say. Her friends were all staring at her. Just then Berry flew down to the beach.

"Sorry I'm late," Berry sang out.

"Berry, you are *always* late," Dash sighed. "We'd better tell you a different start time for

the show. You can't be late for *that* night!"

Berry laughed. "I wouldn't miss my curtain time," she said. "All stars know not to do that."

Dash rolled her eyes. "Well, what have you planned?"

"I am going to sing," Berry proudly announced. "And I am going to make a new dress." She pulled out a small bag from her basket. "I got these amazing jelly-candy stones," she said. She held out her hand to show off the brightly colored round stones. They were sparkling and precious in pinks and purples. "I got them when we were on Meringue Island. I knew they would come in handy one day." She slipped them back into the bag. "I am going to sew them onto my dress. Don't you think that will be a fantastic costume?"

"Delicious," Raina agreed.

Berry was a total fashion fairy. She loved all fashion, glamour, and glitz. She was usually late to meet up because she always had to look perfect, not a hair out of place. Her sense of style was like no other fairy's.

"What are you going to sing?" Melli asked.

Berry grinned. "A lullaby with Lyra," she said. "I love her unicorn songs, and she's taught me a new one to sing. We've been practicing."

Berry's singing with Lyra, the unicorn of Fruit Chew Meadow, made sense to Cocoa. The two spent a lot of time together. She knew their act would be supersweet and Berry's costume would be *sweet-tacular*.

"Are you going to play your licorice-stick, Melli?" Raina asked.

"Yes," Melli said. "I'm playing an old Candy Cotton song. I heard that Candy Cotton is Queen Sweetie's favorite singer."

Cocoa had heard of Candy Cotton. She was a famous lollipop singer. Mocha loved her music. Candy Cotton sang slow, jazzy songs that were popular when her cousin was a young fairy but were still popular around the kingdom. Melli would do a wonderful job playing one of those tunes.

"What are you fairies going to do for the show?" Berry asked, settling down on Raina's pink blanket.

"We're going to do a dance," Dash said. She pointed to Raina and Cocoa.

"Well, I . . . ," Cocoa began to explain.

"Please be in our dance, Cocoa," Raina said.

"Please, we need three fairies," Dash pleaded.

Cocoa looked over at Melli. Melli smiled and shrugged. Somehow Cocoa had a feeling that Melli might have talked to Raina and Dash before Sun Dip. It seemed a little too convenient for them to have thought of a routine for three fairies.

Cocoa wasn't too sure that being in a dance number for a talent show was for her. Her stomach was feeling a little too flip-floppy.

"I'll think about it," Cocoa told her friends.

Raina and Dash shared a look.

Cocoa decided to change the subject. "What is Fruli designing for the scenery?"

"Fruli was such a good choice as stage manager," Berry said. "She is going to make that stage sparkle and shine."

Cocoa knew that Berry loved Fruli the Fruit Fairy. She lived in a large, castle-like home on Meringue Island. Like Berry, she had very good taste in clothes. She was also generous and kind. Cocoa agreed that Fruli was just the one to lead the talent show project.

"She's in charge of making all the backdrops for the acts," Raina said. "That is a huge job."

Berry jumped up. "I think we should help

her," she said. "We can all make some candy and pitch in. Princess Lolli must want the show to be superspecial for her parents."

Cocoa nodded. She felt the same way and wondered how she would be able to help. She listened to her friends brainstorm ideas for the stage. Their excitement was contagious.

"Are you in?" Dash asked Cocoa. Her blue eyes were wide and focused right on Cocoa.

Looking over at Raina and Dash, Cocoa sighed. Maybe she could dance with them. She took a deep breath. "I'd love to dance with you," she said, smiling.

"So mint!" Dash cheered.

"Lickin' lollipops!" Raina exclaimed. "We're going to have a blast."

Melli put her arm around Cocoa. "I knew you'd change your mind. This is going to be *sugar-tastic!*"

Cocoa smiled at Melli, but she couldn't help feeling her wings twitch when she thought about performing onstage.

3

Dancing Divas

For the next week, Cocoa awoke early each morning. She ate her breakfast quickly and headed out to check on her garden. The weather was sunny and bright, and Cocoa got right to work. She pulled the weeds around the seedlings and watered the tiny sprouts. She couldn't wait for the flowers to bloom!

Having patience was the hardest part about growing flowers. Time and again Mocha would tell her that waiting for flowers to bloom was like watching candy ripen on the vine. If you watched all the time, then time moved more slowly.

As Cocoa peered down at the ground, she saw that the chocolate stems were still about the same height as last week. They had to be much taller before the tiny buds would open.

"This is going to take a long time," she said to herself.

Cocoa decided to send a sugar fly message to Mocha. Now that the stems were coming up and buds were beginning to form, she wanted to share the news. Along with her note, she would send a drawing of her garden. She wanted Mocha to see the seedlings' progress.

During Cocoa's last visit, Mocha had also given her a bag of colored pencils. The pencils were in a flowered bag with colorful licorice strings for straps. "This is so you can bring your pencils out to your garden," Mocha had told her. "You can keep me posted on the seedlings' progress."

Stretching out on a rock, Cocoa held her sketch pad in her lap. She loved using her new pencils and was happy with her drawing. When Cocoa finished, she called to a sugar fly. The little fly eagerly took the letter addressed to Mocha at the Royal Palace. No one carried news faster than sugar flies!

"Thank you," Cocoa said to the little fly. She watched the fly buzz off in the direction of the palace.

Cocoa placed her pencils back in the purse. Then she noticed the time. She had a date to meet Raina and Dash in Gummy Forest. She wasn't sure what to expect from their first dance rehearsal.

When Cocoa arrived, her friends were dancing to a Sugar Pops songs. They had chosen "Chocolate Touch," one of Cocoa's favorites. The song had a good beat and she knew all the words.

Their moves were timed perfectly, and not a step—or even a wing—was out of place.

"You look great," Cocoa said at the end of the dance. "I love that song."

"I'm so glad you like the song," Dash told her. She moved closer to Cocoa. She grabbed Cocoa's hands and pulled her. "Let's get started."

"The beginning goes like this," Raina said. She did the steps as she spoke. "First step to the left, then turn, kick, and clap."

Cocoa followed along with her, but she was a few steps behind.

"Why don't you watch first?" Raina suggested. She smiled at Cocoa.

Cocoa sat down and watched Raina and Dash dance. They did a few steps and a couple of twirls at the same time.

Cocoa wasn't sure how she was going to

remember all those steps! The song ended and Cocoa knew her face was showing all her doubt.

"We'll take it slow at first," Dash said.

"I never realized how long that song is," Cocoa mumbled.

"We'll show you. Don't worry," Dash promised.

Cocoa tried her best, but each move was difficult. She couldn't remember the order and couldn't keep on the beat. More than once she bumped into Dash on the turns. She even stepped on Raina's foot three times!

Raina stopped the music. "Maybe we should look at the routine the way I wrote it down," she said. "Sometimes it helps to 'read' the steps."

Cocoa sat down and read the dance steps that Raina had written out. Raina loved books

and often quoted the Fairy Code Book. More than anything, Raina loved words and books. *But this is different,* thought Cocoa.

"Step, step, turn around," Raina said. She clapped her hands to the rhythm of the song.

"Step, step, turn around," Cocoa repeated. But just because she could say the words didn't mean her feet would follow!

"You need to hear the music," Dash said, jumping up. "Cocoa needs to *feel* the music." She gave Raina a sideways glance. "Reading the steps isn't going to help her."

Raina shot Dash a sour look. "She needs to learn the steps," she muttered.

Cocoa didn't like that her two friends were bickering. Raina was all about the steps and the written routine. Dash was more freestyle.

Cocoa's wings drooped. She had no style and, sadly, no rhythm.

"Maybe we should take a break," Cocoa said. She looked back and forth between her friends. She had to change the subject—fast. "What about costumes? Should we wear the same thing?"

"We should wear something that sparkles," Dash said. "A bright icy blue!"

"Rainbow!" Raina exclaimed.

Cocoa's shoulders slumped. Costumes didn't seem to be a safe topic either. "Maybe we should each wear a different color?" Cocoa offered.

"The act needs to have a name," Raina said.

"We could be the Dancing Divas!" Dash shouted.

A smile spread across Raina's face. *"Sweeeet!"*

As Raina and Dash kept talking about the dance, Cocoa thought, *And I am more like a Dancing Disaster.*

CHAPTER

4

Chocolate Change

How's your act coming along?" Berry called as she flew over Gummy Forest. The Fruit Fairy was happy to find that the dancing rehearsal had started. She landed next to Cocoa.

Cocoa wanted to tell Berry about how she couldn't keep up with the steps and how she wasn't sure of the beat, but she just looked away.

"Let's show you!" Dash exclaimed.

Cocoa's stomach did a flip-flop. "Maybe I should just sit this one out," she said.

Raina came over to her. "Really? You'll get the steps, Cocoa," she told her. "Come on. You just need to practice."

Waving her hand in front of her, Cocoa smiled. "No, really, I think you and Dash should be the Dancing Diva *Duo*."

"Are you sure?" Dash asked. "We wanted you to do this with us."

Cocoa was touched her friends seemed so surprised that she wouldn't want to be in the dance with them.

Did they forget how awful I am? she thought.

"I am one hundred chocolate percent sure," Cocoa told them.

Berry moved over on the bench so Cocoa could sit next to her. Dash and Raina took their positions and Cocoa started the Sugar Pops song. Cocoa watched how her friends glided through the dance. They didn't step on each other's toes. They didn't bump into each other. The dance looked fantastic.

"Wow," Berry cheered at the end of the song. "You did a great job with the choreography."

"Bravo!" Cocoa chimed in.

"Now we just need some help with the costumes," Dash said. She grinned at Berry with wide, pleading eyes.

Berry laughed. "I can help you with that,"

she said, taking the hint, "if Raina will give me some of her rainbow gummy jewels she was talking about last week. I would love to work with those. We could come up with extra-sweet costumes."

"I have the gummies here for you already," Raina said. "I had a feeling you'd want to use them." She flew over to a tree stump and pulled out a cloth bag.

Berry clapped her hands. "Sweet strawberries, these are beautiful, Raina." She held the tiny jewels in her hand. "Where did you find these?"

"I was taking a walk with Bella the gummy bear cub, and we stopped for a rest at the edge of Gummy Forest," she said. "These were growing along the shores of the Vanilla Sea."

Dash reached her hand out. "Can I taste one?"

"Oh, Dash, these are much too pretty to eat!" Berry playfully scolded.

Dash might be a small fairy, but her appetite for all candy was huge!

"I have such a sweet idea for these," Berry went on. "I'm excited to make you costumes for the dance."

"You'd make anything look *sweet-tacular*," Cocoa said. She sometimes gave Berry a hard time for being so into fashion, but the truth was, Berry had the talent and flair to carry off any style.

"Tell me some ideas you have for your costumes," Berry said.

As her friends discussed costume ideas,

Cocoa walked to the lake. She bent down and admired the gummy flowers growing there.

Berry came up behind her. "Cocoa, why don't you sing with Lyra and me?" she asked. "I'd love for you to be in the act with us."

Cocoa looked over at Dash and Raina, who were grinning. They had all come over to the lake to talk to her.

"That's a great idea," Raina said.

"Then we can all be in the show," Dash added.

"Just a small chocolate change," Berry giggled. "Please, Cocoa?"

Cocoa bit her lip. "Um, I . . . well, er . . . ," she stumbled.

Berry put out her hand and pulled Cocoa up. "We'll be great," she said. "What do you say?"

Once again Cocoa found she was unable to speak honestly. What was so bad about not wanting to be in a talent show? Why couldn't her friends understand?

"Come to our rehearsal later," Berry said quickly.

It was never easy to say no to the strong-flavored Fruit Fairy!

"Lyra and I are meeting in Fruit Chew Meadow this afternoon," Berry told her. She tilted her head. "Come and see how you feel," she added.

Thankful that Berry wasn't pushing her to make a decision right then and there, Cocoa agreed to go to the rehearsal. At least she would have time to figure out how to break the news to Berry that she couldn't sing. Had Berry never realized that Cocoa always mouthed the words to songs? She couldn't carry a tune at all!

"I have something else to show you fairies," Berry stated proudly. She unfolded a piece of cloth that had been tucked in her basket. "I am making these for the stage lights," she said. The brightly colored light covers were extremely delicate, and Berry handled them with great care.

"Wow, that is *so mint*!" Dash exclaimed. "We can dance under a rainbow of colors!"

"Fruli is doing a great job getting all the fairies to make cool candy decorations for the stage," Berry said.

Cocoa was happy to talk about decorations. Making chocolate decorations was something she could do! She told her friends about the chocolate flowers. "I don't know if they will bloom in time for the show," Cocoa added.

Berry frowned. "Fruli wants all decorations tomorrow," she said. "The dress rehearsal is tonight after Sun Dip. The stage needs to be ready by then."

Standing up, Cocoa fluttered her wings.

"I'd better get back to the garden," she told her friends.

The other fairies all shared a concerned look.

"You could make other chocolate candies for the stage, not just flowers," Raina said.

Cocoa shrugged. "I know, but I am hoping the chocolate rose will bloom." Before her friends could say anything else, Cocoa said a quick good-bye and headed back to Chocolate Woods.

Her singing may not be any better than her dancing . . . but at least she had a little time to figure out how to tell Berry. Right now she wanted to see if the chocolate buds had opened. To her, the flowers blooming would be better than any show opening.

5

Mocha Surprise

Cocoa happily spent the rest of the afternoon in her garden. The tiny buds on the stems were still sealed shut, but if she leaned close, she could see a hint of the chocolate rose petals. The tiny bud was slightly cracked at the top to show off the petals hidden underneath. Cocoa was so relieved. When a bud was showing a bit of the petals, a full bloom was likely to happen soon. The other flowers in the garden had petals peeking out of the buds as well. Soon her garden would be in full bloom! Cocoa wasn't sure if she could wait another day!

Taking out her sketch pad and pencils, Cocoa settled in and began to draw her garden. Drawing helped her relax and forget about the talent show. She loved the way the colors blended on the paper.

Lost in her own world of coloring, Cocoa wasn't aware that someone was watching her.

"Hello, sugar love!" a voice boomed from above.

Cocoa dropped her pencil and looked up in the chocolate oak tree behind her. Sitting on a branch was her cousin Mocha!

"Mocha!" Cocoa squealed. "What are you doing here?" She was so happy to see her. She flew over and gave her a great big hug.

"I thought I would surprise you," Mocha said, smiling. "I had to bring some flower seeds to the Royal Palace Gardens." Her brown eyes shone brightly. "I love an excuse to come to Candy Kingdom and see you! I am glad that I got to sneak over and take a peek at your garden." She flew down off the branch and admired Cocoa's work.

"Look," Cocoa said. She pointed to the opening bud. "I think the flowers are getting ready to burst out."

Mocha smiled. "I knew your seeds would grow," she said. "You are a very fine gardener."

"I did everything you told me," Cocoa said.

"I brought you some cocoa bean shells for the soil," Mocha said. She scooped out the hard, fragrant shells from her basket and sprinkled them around the flowers. "The shells will protect the ground and keep the moisture in," she explained.

Cocoa took a deep breath. "And the shells make my garden smell extra chocolaty! Thank you!"

Mocha leaned over to examine the buds. "I bet these will bloom this week or next," she told Cocoa. "Keep up your weeding and watering, and hope for good weather." She grinned. "The three Ws of gardening."

Cocoa looked down at her feet. "Do you think the flowers will bloom before the talent show? King Crunch and Queen Sweetie are coming to Candy Kingdom, you know."

"I know all about their visit. But in two days?" Mocha asked. She raised her eyebrows high. "That would be unlikely." She smiled at Cocoa. "But not impossible."

Cocoa knew she was asking a lot of her flowers. "All my friends are going to be in the talent show," she said. "I don't really have any talent, Mocha," she added quietly.

"I wouldn't say that, Cocoa," Mocha said. She walked over to the bench, saw Cocoa's pad and pencils, and picked up the drawing. "These sketches are *choc-o-rific*," she said. "You have been working hard."

Cocoa knew Mocha would think anything she did was *choc-o-rific*. She shrugged. "Thank you," she said, "but I wish there were real flowers in my garden, not just buds."

"Ah," Mocha said. She came over and gave Cocoa a squeeze. "Remember, Cocoa Bean, waiting for flowers to bloom is like watching candy ripen on the vine. It goes much faster when you are not watching!" She bent down and kissed Cocoa. "The flowers will come. These drawings are just delicious. You are a very talented artist."

Cocoa stopped and stared at Mocha. *"Talented?"* She had never heard anyone use that word about her! "I also have some paintings inside," Cocoa told her. Mocha followed her inside.

Mocha stood back and admired the paintings. "These are yummy to look at, Cocoa."

"Thanks, Mocha," Cocoa said, smiling. Mocha always had a way of making a moment sweeter.

Just then Cocoa glanced at the clock on her wall. "Oh no!" she moaned. She hadn't realized the time. "I am so late!" she exclaimed. "I am supposed to be in Fruit Chew Meadow right now. I am sorry, Mocha, I really have to fly."

"I understand, sweetie," the older fairy said. "Go ahead. I will see you soon." She waved good-bye. "And keep those pictures coming!" she called to Cocoa. "I love getting sugar fly messages from you. Especially ones with drawings!"

"I will!" Cocoa cried as she flew away.

"Thank you for coming! And for the cocoa bean shells!"

As she raced to Fruit Chew Meadow, Cocoa thought about what Mocha had said about her being a talented artist. She savored the words as if they were a rare and rich chocolate treat.

When Cocoa got to Fruit Chew Meadow, she spotted Berry and Lyra in the far corner. They were already singing. She ducked behind a fruit-chew bush and listened to the beautiful harmonies Berry and Lyra made together. They were singing an old unicorn lullaby with a gentle melody. Cocoa twisted her long hair around one of her fingers. At that very moment, she knew there was no way she could be part of their act.

Luckily, Berry and Lyra didn't notice her, and Cocoa was able to slip away. She knew that if Berry spotted her, she would encourage Cocoa to stay and sing. Cocoa's voice wouldn't blend in nicely with theirs, and she didn't want to ruin the lovely sound they were creating together.

As she took flight, Cocoa sighed. She knew

it was official. She was not going to be part of the talent show. She couldn't dance. She couldn't sing. Maybe she was just like the buds on her chocolate stems—afraid to open and be part of the show.

6

Sweet Music

As Cocoa flew over Chocolate River, she took a deep breath. The smell of fresh chocolate always helped clear her head. The milk chocolate in the river looked so delicious in the afternoon light. Cocoa couldn't resist the urge to dip down for a quick drink.

Happy that no other Chocolate Fairies were

around, Cocoa sat on the bank and dipped her cup into the river. The cool milk chocolate made her relax, and she leaned back and thought about her problem.

She didn't want to be the bitter bits in the "Chocolate Touch" dance or hit all the sour notes in Berry and Lyra's lullaby.

Cocoa took another sip of chocolate. She felt bad that she had snuck away from the song rehearsal, but she didn't know what to say to Berry or to any of her friends. Maybe at Sun Dip tonight she would tell them she'd had second thoughts about being in the show.

It shouldn't be a surprise, thought Cocoa. Berry, Dash, Raina, and Melli were so gifted, they would be relieved not to have her in the show. They all must have thought she was a salted log!

Cocoa gazed up to the sky. Over to the north, she saw Caramel Hills. She wondered what Melli was doing now. Maybe they could make some candy together or play a game . . . anything that had nothing to do with the talent show!

As Cocoa flew over to Caramel Hills, she noticed the chocolate stage on the riverbank.

There were a bunch of fairies working.

Is everyone in Sugar Valley involved in the talent show? she wondered.

When Cocoa arrived at Melli's house, she heard a familiar tune. Melli was playing the Candy Cotton song on her licorice-stick clarinet. It sounded just like the real recording! Cocoa was so impressed with her friend. When the song was over, she knocked on the door.

"Cocoa!" Melli cried. She was very surprised to see the Chocolate Fairy and pushed the door open wider. "Come in," she said. "I was just trying to figure out what to play for the show."

"That sounded super," Cocoa told her.

"Thanks," Melli said, blushing. "It's between that song and this one." She held up another

piece of sheet music. "Can I play this one for you?"

"Sure," Cocoa said. If all she had to do was sit and listen, she could handle that. She sat down on a butterscotch-colored beanbag chair and settled in for a musical treat.

Melli placed the music on her stand and took a deep breath. Cocoa watched how Melli seemed to be a different fairy as she played. She was *really* talented. Cocoa was amazed. Melli had the confidence of a professional musician.

When the song was over, Cocoa applauded. "I vote for that one," she said. "Is that a Candy Cotton song too?"

"Yes," Melli said. "'My Sugar Pie' was one of her early hits."

"King Crunch and Queen Sweetie will love to hear you play. And Princess Lolli will be so pleased," Cocoa assured her. "You are *choc-o-rific*, Melli."

Melli put her clarinet back in the case. "Thank you," she said. "I'm really looking forward to the show." She looked at Cocoa for a moment. "What happened at the song rehearsal?"

Cocoa shook her head. "I didn't go," she said. "I mean, I did go, but I didn't sing." She saw Melli's confused look and tried to explain. "I got there late, and I heard Berry and Lyra singing together. They had such beautiful harmony, I didn't want to ruin their song."

"You wouldn't have ruined the song," Melli said.

"Yes, I would have!" Cocoa said, laughing.

Melli came over and sat on the beanbag chair next to Cocoa's. "Well, you'll find another act." She tapped her finger on her chin. "Let's find out what Cara is going to do."

Rolling her eyes, Cocoa pleaded with Melli. "Sure as sugar, your sister will play her flute," she said.

"Oh, Cocoa," Melli said with a heavy sigh.

Cocoa stood up. "I'm tired of talking about the show. Can't I just be in the audience and enjoy it that way? Let's do something else. How about if we design some new chocolate-caramel candy?"

"Or let's make some candy for the stage decorations," Melli said. "I saw Fruli today at the Royal Gardens. She wants all the Candy

Fairies to make candy decorations for the scenery."

"I saw some fairies working there today," Cocoa said. "What did you have in mind?"

"I was thinking we could make some chocolate-caramel-colored stars to pop up around the edge of the stage," Melli said. "What do you think?"

Cocoa shrugged. "Okay," she replied.

"They can be uscd as party treats after the show," Melli said, giggling.

Cocoa agreed. Although making the candy was still about the talent show, at least she didn't have to perform!

The two fairies headed outside to gather some caramel for the stage stars.

"How is your garden?" Melli askcd as they

worked. "Will the flowers be ready for the show?"

Cocoa thought about the timing. "Maybe," she said. "I'm still waiting for the buds to open. My cousin Mocha came by for a visit today. She thought it was possible, but she couldn't be sure."

"Wow, wouldn't that be something if you gave the flowers to Queen Sweetie?" Melli asked.

"It would be something," Cocoa said. "But the buds haven't opened on any of the stems. I don't think the flowers are going to bloom in time."

"Too bad," Melli replied.

"Mocha keeps telling me to be patient," Cocoa said. "But it's so hard."

Suddenly Melli blurted out, "It just won't be the same if you aren't in the show with us! Please think again about being in an act."

Cocoa blushed pink. She thought about sitting in the audience alone while her friends were all backstage. She fluttered her wings. Maybe Melli was right. She *would* feel left out.

"Okay," she said. "I'll talk to Berry again at Sun Dip," she said sadly.

"Cheer up," Melli said. "This is going to be great fun. You'll see." She waved some glitter over their candies. "The magic of the theater," she said.

Cocoa gave Melli a smile, but she wasn't feeling any magic at all.

"Why don't you drop these candies off at the stage on your way home," Melli said.

"Maybe you'll be inspired. The stage is *choc-o-rific*!"

Cocoa sighed. She didn't think seeing the chocolate stage was going to help her be good at any act. "Sure," she said anyway. She packed up the candy in a box.

At least she knew that along with her fairy friends, her chocolate-caramel candies would be stars onstage.

CHAPTER

7

Painting Chocolate

Cocoa left Caramel Hills with a box full of colorful, glittery chocolate-caramel stars. When she arrived, there were a few other Candy Fairies dropping off candies, and the stage was looking *sweet-tacular*. Cocoa was impressed with all the candy touches. There were rows of sugar candies sewn on beautiful pink cotton candy sheets for the curtains. Against the wall at the back, colorful gumdrops and licorice strips created a sparkling rainbow. And in each corner were giant swirl lollipops.

"Hi!" Fruli called when she saw Cocoa. She waved, and Cocoa landed next to her. "Just what we need, a Chocolate Fairy!" Fruli exclaimed. "It's so good to see you!"

For the first time in days, Cocoa stood up a little straighter. She knew how to be a Chocolate Fairy. It felt good to be needed for a talent that came naturally. "Just don't ask me to sing or dance," she said, smiling.

"Not today," Fruli replied. "We have too much to do here with the setup." Fruli was wearing a beautiful flower dress. As always,

she looked as if she could have been in a fashion magazine. She was also holding a large scroll and a long licorice pen. Being in charge of building a stage and putting on a show was a huge responsibility. Fruli pointed to the corner of the stage. "We need more chocolate over here. We should have made the sides wider. And we need to do this quickly. Tonight is the dress rehearsal!"

Cocoa saw that the stage was narrow on the sides. There was not enough room for more than two fairies to stand.

"Do you think you can help make some chocolate strips to build the floor?" Fruli asked. "We need more chocolate—and fast."

"Chocolate strips, coming right up," Cocoa said.

"Great!" Fruli exclaimed. "I am so glad you came by. I really needed your help."

Cocoa grinned. "I came to drop off these chocolate-caramel stars. Melli and I made them today." She handed her the box of colorful candies. "We thought the stars would look yummy and add to the scenery."

Fruli peered inside the box. "Scrumptious! We can line these around the edge of the stage. Thank you. Supersweet of you!"

"This place looks *choc-o-rific*!" Cocoa said.

"Everyone has worked so hard," Fruli told her. "Plus, the show is going to be a great hit. Are you singing or dancing?"

Cocoa bit her lip and then sighed with relief when a Fruit Fairy rushed over, needing Fruli's help.

"Sorry, Cocoa," Fruli called over her shoulder. "I have to fly. Thanks again for helping out with the chocolate!"

Cocoa was relieved she didn't have to explain to Fruli why she couldn't be part of the show. As hard as she tried, she couldn't shake off the feeling of not wanting to perform. She was happy to start making the chocolate strips, and in no time, she had made the stage wider. Cocoa had to admit she was enjoying helping out. Melli was right about being part of the fun. But as she stood on the stage to make sure the chocolate strips were secure, she had no desire to be in the spotlight!

"Cocoa," Fruli said, flying up to her. "Berry told me you are growing chocolate flowers like the ones in the gardens at the Royal Palace."

"I am," Cocoa said. "My cousin Mocha gave me the seeds. My flowers haven't bloomed yet. Right now there are just tiny buds."

"Oh," Fruli sighed. "I was hoping to decorate the stage with the flowers. Queen Sweetie loves all flowers—but especially chocolate roses."

Cocoa hung her head. "I know," she said. "I thought about that too."

"That's okay," Fruli said. "Thanks so much for making the stage wider. This is going to be a *delicious* show!"

"I'll see you later," Cocoa said. She took off for Chocolate Woods. She wanted to check on her flower buds. Maybe they were ready!

But when Cocoa arrived at her garden, she

was disappointed once again. The buds were still closed.

Maybe the flowers have stage fright, she thought.

Cocoa went inside and got her pad and pencils. She came back outside, found a comfy spot, and started sketching the flower buds. Then she had an even better idea. Back inside she went to get her paints.

As the sun was dipping down behind the Frosted Mountains, Cocoa painted what she imagined her garden would look like once the flowers bloomed. With each stroke, she painted large, beautiful flowers with bright, juicy colors.

Her white and dark chocolate paints were from Cupcake Lake in Cake Kingdom, the neighboring kingdom ruled by Princess Lolli's

sister, Princess Sprinkle. The paints were dyed different colors, but Cocoa's favorite was the milk chocolate. She used that shade for the chocolate rose. Cocoa usually decorated chocolates with her special icing paints, but using these paints made her flowers seem real. This way the paintings were made not just with sugar, but with chocolate!

If only my garden really looked like this, she thought.

Cocoa gazed at her paintings in the soft moonlight. She loved how the painted flowers looked on the canvases . . . and smelled! Then she realized that if there was moonlight, Sun Dip had passed.

"Oh no!" she exclaimed. She had been working so hard, she had forgotten all about Sun Dip! She knew by now her friends would be gone from Red Licorice Lake.

"Sour sticks," she sighed. It seemed just as well. This way she didn't have to talk—or hear—about the talent show again. Plus, they were probably now all at the Chocolate River stage for the dress rehearsal. The big show was tomorrow night.

Cocoa brought her paintings inside and fell asleep. She dreamed she was playing in a lush, sweet chocolate rose garden. Her dream turned from sweet to sour when the salty old troll who lived under the bridge in Black Licorice Swamp appeared. Any dream involving Mogu the troll was sure to be horrible. He swept through her garden, stomping and eating her flowers.

"Nooooo!" Cocoa screamed.

She startled herself awake and realized that she had been dreaming. Once she was aware that Mogu was just in her dream, she relaxed and drifted back to a dream filled with sweet chocolate roses.

8

Showstopper!

A forceful thumping woke Cocoa up the next morning. Half asleep, she opened her door to find her four friends gathered in her doorway.

"Cocoa!" Melli cried. She leaped toward her and gave her a giant squeeze. "There you are!"

"I told you she was probably sleeping," Berry

said with her arms crossed over her chest. "All that worrying, and she is fine!"

"Huh?" Cocoa said. She squinted up at the bright sun. "What's going on?"

"Well, sweet mint leaves!" Dash exclaimed. She pushed through to grab Cocoa's hand. "I am so happy you are here. I thought for sure Mogu had taken you!"

Cocoa rubbed her eyes. "What are you talking about?" she said.

"Where were you last night?" Raina asked. "You skipped Sun Dip, and then you missed the news about Mogu this morning."

Cocoa stretched her wings out and yawned big. "Mogu?" she asked. "I had a dream about him last night."

"I wish this was a dream," Berry mumbled.

Any news involving him was sure to be bittersweet. "What happened with Mogu?" Cocoa asked.

"He *ate* the stage!" Dash blurted out.

"You're not serious, are you?" Cocoa asked. "Even Mogu couldn't eat *that* much, could he?"

"He did. Now we don't know if there is going to be a talent show," Melli answered.

"We should have known he'd come around. We should have guarded the stage." Cocoa looked down at her doorstep. On the ground was a stack of sugar fly notes. "I guess I didn't hear the sugar flies buzzing last night," she said softly. "Or earlier this morning. I stayed up late painting and didn't hear a thing."

"I am just glad you are okay," Melli said. "We were nervous that you might have been at the chocolate stage when Mogu came up Chocolate River."

"Plus, we missed you last night during the dress rehearsal," Raina said. "It wasn't the same without you there."

Cocoa looked at her friends' faces. They all looked so concerned. "I thought you'd all be so busy with the dress rehearsal that you wouldn't miss me," she said.

"What?" her friends said at the same time.

Cocoa walked back into her room. "I can't be in a talent show," she muttered. "I've been trying to tell all of you that, but I wasn't sure how." She turned around to see that her friends had followed her inside. "You've been very nice to include me, but I would ruin any act. And I can't do that to Princess Lolli or her parents. Their visit is much too important."

"You are joking, right?" Melli asked.

"I'm . . . I'm afraid that . . ." Cocoa paused as she searched for the right words.

"That doesn't sound like you, Cocoa!" Dash interrupted her. "You are the bravest Candy Fairy I know. You faced Mogu and tricked him in Black Licorice Swamp! How could you be afraid of being in a show?"

Cocoa shook her head and smiled at Dash. "It's not stage fright," she said. "I am afraid . . ." She paused and then continued. "That I don't have any talent to perform." She sighed. Finally Cocoa was able to be honest with her friends.

"Cocoa," Raina said, "we just want you to be with us. It's not every day that the king and queen come to Candy Kingdom. We thought it would be fun to be in the show together."

Melli moved closer to Cocoa. "I didn't realize you really didn't want to perform," she said.

"You should have told us," Berry said. She squinted and looked past Cocoa. "Are these your paintings?" she asked, looking at the freshly painted canvases hanging to dry. She walked slowly up and down, examining each one.

"You *were* busy last night! These flowers are incredible," Raina said.

"Is this what your garden looks like?" Berry asked.

"Not yet," Cocoa mumbled.

Dash moved closer to the paintings. "Holy peppermint!" she said. "These smell like real flowers. How did you do that?"

Cocoa shifted her feet. "I used my chocolate

paints," she said. "The buds in the garden haven't opened yet, and I wanted the flowers to seem real."

"These paintings are amazing," Raina said. "That was extra-creative."

"And original," Melli added.

"I think art is your true talent, Cocoa," Berry said with a smile.

Cocoa blushed. "Thank you," she replied. Creating the art had made her so happy. She was glad her friends liked her paintings.

Through the open door, a sugar fly flew in. The tiny fly landed on Cocoa's shoulder and chirped. He flapped his wings a few times excitedly and dropped a letter in her hand. As fast he had flown in, he flew back outside.

"Sure as sugar, he was very happy to see

you!" Melli said, giggling. "Finally you were around to get a message."

Cocoa opened the letter and read it quickly. "Fruli needs us to come at once," she said. "She guessed that you'd all be here."

"Do you think she is going to have to cancel the show?" Melli asked.

"I hope not," Berry said.

"We don't have that much time," Dash said. "The king and queen are arriving today, and the show is tonight."

Cocoa folded the letter and slipped it into her pocket. "Let's go see what the damage is," she said. "Mogu makes everything a bitter mess. That troll is not neat and tidy about eating chocolate."

"Poor Princess Lolli!" Melli moaned. "She

was so excited when she came to the dress rehearsal last night." She turned to Cocoa. "Everything was perfect! She was proud of us and our work."

"Don't dip your wings in syrup yet," Berry snapped. "No one said anything about canceling."

Dash rolled her eyes. "Not having a stage is a showstopper for sure!"

"Let's go see what Fruli needs," Cocoa said. She was feeling bad about missing Sun Dip and then sleeping through all the news about Mogu's feast. "Maybe we can do something to save the event."

The five fairies took off toward Chocolate River, unsure of what they'd find . . . or of whether the show would go on.

CHAPTER

9

Chocolate Tracks

When the friends arrived at Chocolate River, they saw a sad sight. The candy stage had been torn apart. There were chocolate pieces along the shore and bits of candy everywhere. Mogu and the Chuchies had definitely been there—the chocolate mess was their handiwork! The Chuchies followed Mogu

everywhere and loved to eat candy just as much as he did.

Cocoa's heart melted. Yesterday the stage had been amazingly decorated with patterns of luscious candies and stunning gumdrop lights.

"It looks like a stampede of wild unicorns ran through here," Melli said sadly.

"No unicorn would ever do this much damage," Berry replied. She shook her head as she looked around. "This has Mogu and his Chuchies written all over it."

"Mogu is lying somewhere with an enormous bellyache," Raina said.

"Serves him right," Dash huffed. "He has ruined everything!"

Cocoa slowly turned around. "Not really," she said. "I think we can rebuild the stage in time."

"Oh, Cocoa," Fruli said, overhearing Cocoa. She flew over to her and grabbed her hand. "Do you really think we can?"

Cocoa felt so sorry for Fruli—and all the Candy Fairies who had put so much work into making the stage. She knew there was no time to re-create the decorations that were on the stage yesterday, but at least they could rebuild the stage for the performance. She felt all eyes on her.

"Sure as sugar!" Cocoa exclaimed. "Come on, let's get working." She smiled at her friends. "Let's split up and have some fairies clean up the mess and the others start building the stage."

"Sounds good to me," Fruli said. "Thank you, Cocoa."

Cocoa couldn't wait to get to work. She and two other Chocolate Fairies created long strips of chocolate. A team of Candy Fairies joined together to build up the stage. After a few hours of making chocolate, the stage was finally rebuilt. It was not as wide or as high as before, but at least there would be a space to perform.

Fruli stood at center stage. "This was a bittersweet day," she told the crowd of Candy Fairies. "This morning I wasn't sure we'd even be able to have a show at all." She smiled at the fairies around her. "But now, after all your efforts, the show will go on!"

Princess Lolli flew up onstage next to Fruli. She gave her a tight squeeze. "Thank you, Fruli," she said. "This morning after the Mogu feast, I wasn't sure we'd be able to get this stage up in time. I sent a few palace guards to deal with Mogu and the Chuchies. Their behavior is not acceptable, and their greediness almost put an end to this event. Your dedication and that of all the Candy Fairies make me so proud.

My parents have just arrived at the castle, and we're all looking forward to this evening and watching the talent show."

"Our show is in two hours!" Fruli gasped, looking at her watch. "We've got to fly, Princess Lolli! There is still so much to be done!"

Princess Lolli laughed. "Thank you," she said. She waved to everyone and then headed back to the castle. "See you soon!" she called.

"We don't have time to decorate," Fruli said to Berry. "But at least we have a stage."

"But what are we going to do about scenery? It's almost showtime," Melli said.

"I guess we'll have to do without a backdrop," Fruli said.

Suddenly a huge grin spread across Melli's face. "I have a *choc-o-rific* idea!" she cried. She grabbed Cocoa and pulled her aside to speak to her alone. Cocoa wasn't sure what Melli was thinking, but she knew her friend was extra-excited. Melli's wings were flapping so fast her feet didn't touch the ground.

"What? What is it?" Cocoa asked.

Melli couldn't speak. All she could do was flap her wings!

"Melli," Cocoa said to her, "calm down. Take a deep breath."

After a few deep breaths, Melli finally put her feet on the ground. "Cocoa, what about your chocolate rose paintings?" she blurted out.

"My chocolate rose paintings?" Cocoa asked.

"We could hang the paintings you made

last night around the stage," Melli said, jumping up and down. "Wouldn't that look absolutely *sugar-tastic*?"

Cocoa looked up at the stage and then back at Melli. She wasn't sure how her paintings would look. They were not as glittery as the hundreds of pieces of candy that had lined the stage yesterday. And those paintings were just for her and Mocha. She had never thought about displaying them for everyone to see.

"Please?" Melli begged. Her wings started flapping uncontrollably again.

"Let's ask Fruli," Cocoa said.

Before Cocoa could say another word, Melli flew over to Fruli. Fruli nodded, then hugged Melli, and then the two fairics rushcd back over to Cocoa, large grins on their faces.

"Your paintings sound like delicious decorations for the stage," Fruli told Cocoa. "We'd love to have them. Remember, Queen Sweetie loves chocolate roses, so this is just icing on the cake!"

"Double-delicious chocolate icing," Dash added.

"And the paintings are made of chocolate," Berry said. "Fruli, you'll love the art. Cocoa used her chocolate paints."

Cocoa felt her face start to get as red as a cinnamon sucker. "I'll go get the paintings, Fruli, and then you can decide."

"I am sure I will love them," Fruli replied. She turned to the rest of the Candy Fairies. "Now, everyone, into your costumes, please! It's just about showtime!"

Cocoa raced back home to get her artwork. As she thought of her paintings being center stage, she smiled. To her, that was the *real* icing on the cake!

10

Pure Talent

Just as quickly as she had flown home, Cocoa returned to Chocolate River. There was excitement everywhere: Some Candy Fairies were practicing their acts and others were still getting ready. Fairies put sugar sparkles in their hair and strawberry lipstick on their lips. Some of the costumes were dazzling!

Cocoa spotted four empty thrones in the audience. Those chairs were reserved for Princess Lolli and the royal visitors. She glanced up at the stage. It was not as elaborate as before, but at least there was a stage.

"Oh, Cocoa," Fruli said. She rushed over to Cocoa, nearly toppling her over. She looked down at Cocoa's hands. "I'm so glad our scenery is here!"

"Wait, you haven't even seen the paintings yet," Cocoa told her as she handed Fruli the canvases.

Fruli carefully unrolled them and was silent.

Oh no, Cocoa thought. *She doesn't like them!*

Cocoa found her voice. "I'll take them back home, Fruli. Don't worry. You don't have to use them."

"Not use them? These painting are even more sensational than I imagined!" Fruli exclaimed. "You have saved the day!" She hugged Cocoa. "Across the back of the stage I put up a licorice rope for you to clip each of the paintings to. The flowers will make an ideal backdrop for all the acts."

"Okay," Cocoa said. She smiled from ear to ear.

"I'll help you," Melli offered. She came up behind Cocoa and gave her shoulder a tap. "I'm ready for my solo, so I have time."

"Oh, Melli," Cocoa said, looking her friend

up and down. Melli was wearing an all-pink tank dress with pink sugar candies around the neck and waist. "You look *sugar-tastic*! I love your outfit."

"Thanks," Melli said. She touched her puffy skirt gently. "I wanted to wear pink since that was Candy Cotton's signature color. Whenever she sang, she *always* wore a pink dress."

Cocoa smiled. "You are *bubble gum–tastic*!" she giggled. "And I know you will sound great too." She gathered up her paintings. "Come on, let's get these onstage!"

The two friends worked together quickly to hang the paintings before the curtain opened.

"Places, everyone!" Fruli called. "The royal family is about to make their entrance!"

There was a scrambling of fairies as they all scattered to their positions backstage. Cocoa went over to Berry, Raina, and Dash. Berry was putting last-minute touches on Raina's and Dash's dresses.

"I know you are all going to be stars," Cocoa said. "And your costumes are supersweet."

Berry secured the final rainbow-gummy jewel on Raina's collar. "Thank you," she said. "And, Cocoa, your paintings are amazing. Everyone is talking about how the stage looks *choc-o-rific!*"

"Art is her special talent," Melli said, beaming at her friend.

"And making chocolate!" Dash added, tapping the solid chocolate stage with her toe.

"For a fairy who didn't believe she had any talent, you sure saved the talent show!" Raina said, giving her a hug.

"I'm going to go sit in the audience now," Cocoa said, blushing. "I can't wait to *watch*." She laughed and hugged each of her friends. "Mocha says that Candy Cotton always used to say, 'Let's give 'em some extra sugar!' Then she'd go onstage and knock everyone out with her voice. You are all going to be a hit. A show with extra sugar!"

"Thanks for everything, Cocoa," Melli said.

Just as Cocoa took her seat, the caramel trumpets blared and the procession of the royal family began. The king and queen came in first and then Princess Sprinkle and Princess Lolli. The family members were each

wearing a crown and their finest royal jewelry.

Princess Lolli winked at Cocoa as she passed by, and Cocoa felt so proud.

From the seat behind her, Cocoa felt a tap on her shoulder. "Cocoa Bean, the paintings are wonderful. I am so glad you are sharing them."

Cocoa smiled and told her cousin what had happened and how her paintings had come to be center stage.

"We're in for a treat!" Mocha cheered as the lights dimmed.

The stage went dark. Then all of Cocoa's paintings were lit with a large spotlight.

There was a roar of applause. Cocoa was so embarrassed. She was glad that no one could see her!

The cast of fairies all performed well. Dash

and Raina didn't miss a beat, and their dance was a complete hit. Melli's song took everyone by surprise. Her music made everyone tap their toes and flutter their wings. The last act of the show was Berry and Lyra's duet. The lullaby, "Sweet and True," brought tears to the queen's eyes. And Cocoa couldn't take her eyes off Berry's dress with the dazzling jelly candy stones sewn around the waist.

At the end of the show, King Crunch and Queen Sweetie flew over to Cocoa.

"I heard you are the artist who created those *choc-o-rific* paintings onstage," Queen Sweetie said. "Do you think King Crunch and I could have one of those paintings to hang in the Royal Palace?" she asked. "I'd love to put it in the garden room."

Cocoa was so stunned that she couldn't answer. Her mouth just hung open and no sound came out.

"She'd love that," Melli said for her friend. She flew up beside Cocoa and took her hand. Berry, Raina, and Dash circled around her as well.

"Excellent," King Crunch said, smiling. He leaned down to Cocoa. "You take after Mocha, yes?" he said. "She has a real talent for growing flowers, and you have a talent for painting them."

"Cocoa also has a garden," Berry said.

"And she's growing chocolate roses," Dash blurted out.

Queen Sweetie smiled. "Chocolate roses in Sugar Valley? I'd enjoy seeing them," she said.

Cocoa whispered into Melli's ear, then turned to the king and queen. "Excuse us, please. We must check on something, but we will be right back."

Queen Sweetie and King Crunch looked at each other and smiled. "We were going to the party at Candy Castle. Princess Lolli has invited all the fairies to come for some sweet treats."

"*So mint!* Don't worry, we'll be there," Dash cried.

Everyone laughed and promised to meet up later at the castle.

Cocoa and her friends flew back to her home. She needed to see if the roses had bloomed. With all her heart, she wished that at least one bud had opened.

As the fairies approached her garden, Cocoa almost started to cry. There, in the middle of her garden, was a chocolate rose! The center flower was open. Her wish had come true!

"Now, that is one delicious-looking blossom," Dash said, sniffing the flower.

"Hot chocolate!" Cocoa exclaimed. "I did it! I really did it!"

"Pure talent," Raina said.

Cocoa bent down and smelled the fresh flower. She had never smelled anything so sweet. In a flash, she knew what she wanted to do with it.

"Thank you," Cocoa said. She reached down and cut the flower's stem.

"What are you doing?" Dash asked.

Cocoa smiled. "Growing flowers is a gift,"

she said. "And I know just the fairy I'd like to give this to."

"But you already gave Queen Sweetie a painting," Melli said.

"I wasn't thinking of the queen," Cocoa said. "I was thinking of someone else."

Her friends looked at one another. They weren't sure what Cocoa was thinking.

Back at the Royal Gardens, the party was in full swing. Trays of candies and cakes were served. Princess Sprinkle had brought mini cupcakes with chocolate flowers from Cake Kingdom for the occasion.

Cocoa flew a little ahead of her friends. She was searching the crowd. There were fairies from all kingdoms. Royal Palace fairies, Cake Fairies, and Candy Fairies were all enjoying the delicious treats and the festive party.

Finally Cocoa spotted the fairy she had been looking for.

"I would like to present you with my very first chocolate rose," Cocoa said. She handed the flower to Mocha.

Mocha's eyes widened. She gasped and put her hand to her mouth. "Cocoa Bean!" she cried. "This is the sweetest rose. What a royally chocolate gift from a truly talented Candy Fairy!"

Cocoa giggled, and her friends circled around her. The chocolate rose was the grand finale to a supersweet show.

FIND OUT

WHAT HAPPENS IN

Melli the Caramel Fairy swooped down to the sugar sand beach at Red Licorice Lake. The sun was slightly above the top of Frosted Mountains. She knew she was early for Sun Dip and that her friends wouldn't be there for a while. Sun Dip didn't officially start until the sun sank below the Frosted Mountains. Melli fluttered her wings. She couldn't wait to share her news!

Spreading her blanket, Melli smiled to herself. She had made fresh caramel hearts for a Sun Dip snack and displayed them on a plate. Sun Dip was her favorite time of day. The colorful sunset in Sugar Valley was the perfect time to be with friends. And Melli had the four best friends in the world.

She didn't have to wait too long for her Chocolate Fairy friend Cocoa to arrive. Cocoa's golden wings were easy to spot in the late afternoon light.

"Hi Cocoa!" Melli called.

"I thought I was going to be first today," Cocoa said. She looked at her friend. "You look like you are bursting with some sweet news."

Melli giggled. "I am!" she squealed. "The most delicious news!"

"Hold on!" Raina the Gummy Fairy cried from above. "*I* have the most scrumptious news of all!"

Dash the Mint Fairy whizzed past Raina and landed next to Melli. "Gee, everyone is extra early today," she said. "What's the great occasion?"

"Someone has news to share," Cocoa said, nodding to Melli and Raina.

"Well, spill!" Dash said as she settled down on Melli's blanket. "Please don't tell me we have to wait for Berry."

Berry the Fruit Fairy was almost always late to events. Her friends knew this about her and expected her to be the last one to arrive.

"She's probably trying on some new outfit," Dash said. Dash was more interested in sledding and speed racing than all the fashions that Berry liked to talk about.

"Maybe," Cocoa said. She looked over at Melli. "I don't think Melli and Raina are going to be able to wait. Go ahead, Melli."

"Hey!" Raina shouted. "I have huge, huge news!"

Dash pointed her wings to Melli. "But Melli was here before you. She should share first."

Sitting up straight, Melli grinned. "Well," she said slowly. She wanted to savor the moment. "Princess Lolli wanted to work on a new dipping technique during the caramel harvest," Melli said, "and she chose me to help!" Her wings flapped and she lifted off the blanket. "I am going to Candy Castle in a couple of weeks so I can meet with her. Today I have been trying different kinds of caramel for the dip."

Cocoa flew over to her friend and gave her a tight squeeze. "I am so proud of you!" she said.

"You are so lucky," Dash told her. "It's not often that you get alone time with Princess Lolli."

"I know." Melli giggled. "I can't wait."

Raina smiled. "That's great, Melli."

Dash looked down at the plate in front of Melli. "Are these fresh caramel?" she asked.

Melli laughed. Dash might be the smallest fairy, but she had the largest appetite. "Yes," she replied. "I couldn't use this batch for the dipping because the caramel was too hard, but it was perfect for shaping hearts."

"Yum!" Dash said. "I think that I am going to love this special project of yours," she added.

"I will be making lots of caramel," Melli said proudly.

Raina stood up. "Now it is time for my news!" she exclaimed. "I'm sorry Berry still isn't here, but you are not going to believe this announcement."

Raina took a deep breath. "I was at Candy Castle this morning," she said, "and I saw this!" She took out a copy of the *Daily Scoop*. "It's a special edition because this news is so delicious!"

On the front page of the newspaper was a large photo of Princess Lolli and a fairy named Prince Scoop. The headline across the top of the paper read, "A Royal Engagement!"